For Fred and his daddy, who always
find friends wherever they go ~ G.D.

For Phil and Jasper. Life is always
lovely when they come along, too.
With love ~ C.J-I.

tiger tales
5 River Road, Suite 128, Wilton, CT 06897
Published in the United States 2020
Originally published in Great Britain 2020
by Little Tiger Press Ltd.
Text by Georgiana Deutsch
Text copyright © 2020 Little Tiger Press Ltd.
Illustrations copyright © 2020 Cally Johnson-Isaacs
ISBN-13: 978-1-68010-226-0
ISBN-10: 1-68010-226-5
Printed in China
LTP/1400/3124/0420

For more insight and activities,
visit us at www.tigertalesbooks.com

Along Came A Fox

by
Georgiana Deutsch

Illustrated by
Cally Johnson-Isaacs

tiger tales

It was just the right kind of night for
finding fireflies, and Bramble was ready.
Silvery moon? Yep!
Sparkly stars? So many!

Unfortunately, Bramble didn't have
a clue where fireflies hide.

In that scratchy bush?
Nope.

How about under this log?

"EEEK!" squeaked Hazel.
"You startled me!"

"I'm sorry!" whispered Bramble,
not very quietly. "I'm looking
for fireflies!"

"Try the lake," hooted Twig,
who knew **everything**.

"And wait for me!" Hazel called.
"I want to see fireflies, too!"

Bramble scrambled down the misty, twisty path. Hazel tiptoed behind, through the creepy, crooked shadows. "Spooky!" she shivered.

"Hurry up!" laughed Bramble.
Because foxes don't
get scared . . .

. . . do they?

"YIKES! A FOX!
WATCH OUT!" cried
Bramble as she tumbled
head-over-tail and landed
SPLAT! on her bottom.

Poor Bramble.
How embarrassing!

"That fox scared me!" grumped Bramble. She stomped back to the water and growled, "You're a VERY RUDE FOX!"

"You're a VERY RUDE FOX!
RUDE FOX! RUDE FOX! RUDE FOX!"
came the reply.
"I'M rude?!" sputtered Bramble.
"It was YOU who was rude!"
Hazel squeezed her eyes shut.
It was starting to get too loud.

Bramble bristled her whiskers.
"There's no room for rude foxes
in this forest!" she barked.
"Why don't you GO AWAY!"

"GO AWAY! GO AWAY!
GO AWAY!" the other
fox echoed.

"That's IT!" snapped Bramble,
her nose in the air. "I'm
going to tell Twig!"

And with that, she stormed back
into the forest, with Hazel
hurrying after her.

Bramble told Twig everything.
Twig listened and nodded in
all the right places.

But then Twig said something very unexpected.
"I wonder what made that fox so upset. Let's
go back to the lake together and ask him."

"I'm sure it wasn't this dark last time!" shivered Hazel.
"The moon is hiding behind the clouds," Twig explained.
She really did know everything.

Bramble was very quiet. "I got angry first,"
she whispered to herself. "Maybe that's what
made the other fox angry."

The lake was still. Bramble edged closer.
But when she peered into the water, she saw . . .

. . . NOTHING!

"The fox has VANISHED!" Bramble cried sadly. "I wanted to make friends, and now it's too late!"

Hazel didn't like to see Bramble upset.
She gave her a prickly hug. "Don't be sad.
We might still see some fireflies!"

But as the moon peeked out from behind the
clouds, they saw something EVEN BETTER . . . .

"THE FOX IS BACK!" Bramble beamed.
"And he's SMILING, TOO!"
Hazel laughed. "He brought FRIENDS!"
she squeaked, waving wildly.

"It just goes to show," nodded Twig, "that we should treat others the way we want to be treated. Tonight you gave that fox your smile, and that's exactly how friendships begin."

Bramble knew Twig was right. As usual. "FOX!" she cried, bouncing in the air. **"LET'S BE FRIENDS!"**

"LET'S BE FRIENDS!" laughed the
other fox. "LET'S BE FRIENDS!
LET'S BE FRIENDS!"

It was the perfect night for
finding all kinds of things . . . .

New friends? Three!
Fluttering fireflies? Too many to count!